CAITCH

D1437264

The Dinosaur Who Lost His ROAR

Russell Punter

Illustrated by Andy Elkerton

Reading Consultant: Alison Kelly
Roehampton University

This is a story about five
dinosaurs –

Sid,

Spike,

Ross,

Ollie

and Rex.

Sid lived in the middle of
a big forest.

He liked living in the forest. He liked

crashing

through bushes.

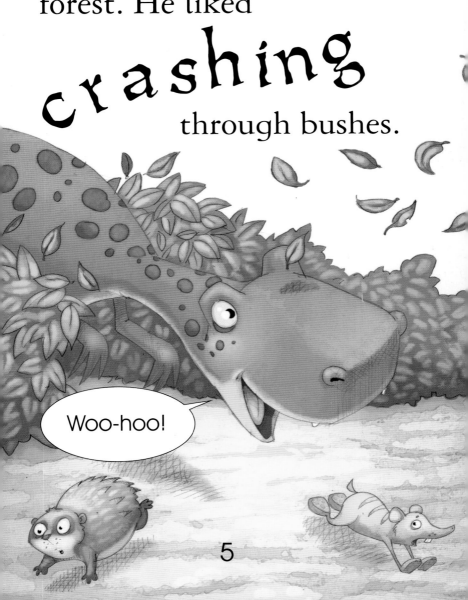

Woo-hoo!

And he liked

splashing

in the river.

Wa-hay!

But, most of all, Sid liked
scaring other dinosaurs.

ROAR!

He had the loudest roar
of all.

One day, Sid went for a walk.

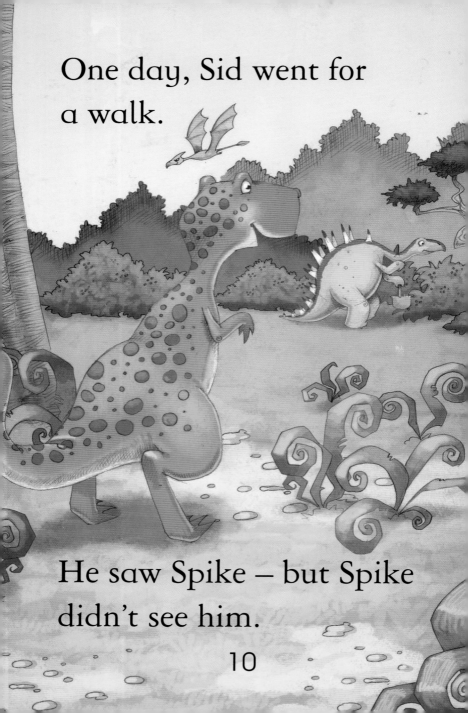

He saw Spike – but Spike didn't see him.

Spike was picking berries.

Mmm, these look juicy.

Sid crept up behind Spike, and gave a...

ROAR!

Splat! Spike got covered in squashy berries.

"Ha, ha," laughed Sid.

"That's not funny, Sid,"
said Spike.

Sid just grinned and
stomped on his way.

14

Ross was catching fish.

Come here,
little fishies.

15

Sid crept up behind Ross,
and gave a... ROAR!

Splash! Ross fell into the water.

"Ha, ha," laughed Sid. "That's not funny, Sid," said Ross.

Sid just grinned and
stomped on his way.

Hee hee!

Ollie was collecting eggs
for her dinner.

I'll have fried
eggs tonight.

Sid crept up behind Ollie, and gave a...

ROAR!

Crack! Eggs went everywhere.

"Ha, ha," laughed Sid. "That's not funny, Sid," said Ollie.

Sid just grinned and stomped on his way.

Ho ho!

When Sid got home, his throat hurt.

The next day, Sid went
for another walk.

He saw Spike picking
berries.

Sid crept up behind Spike
and gave a...

CROAK!

Spike laughed.

Ha ha, Sid.
You've lost your roar.
You can't scare me
any more!

Sid went red in the face
and tiptoed away.

Sid came to the river.
Ross was fishing.

Sid's throat hurt. But he
still wanted to roar.

He crept up behind Ross
and gave a...

CROAK!

Ross laughed.

Ha ha, Sid.
You've lost your roar.
You can't scare me
any more!

Sid went red in the face
and tiptoed away.

Sid came to the tall trees.
Ollie was collecting eggs.

Sid's throat still hurt.
But he wanted to roar.

He crept up behind Ollie
and gave a...

CROAK!

Ollie laughed.

Ha ha, Sid.
You've lost your roar.
You can't scare me
any more!

Sid went red and ran all
the way home.

Sid didn't like being laughed at. It felt bad.

He didn't like having a sore throat either.

So he ate a
spoonful of
honey,

drank some
warm water

and went to bed.

The next day, Sid's throat was better.

He decided to visit Spike, Ross and Ollie.

"I'll say sorry for scaring them," he thought.

Then we can be friends.

Sid went to the berry bushes – but Spike wasn't there.

That's odd.

He went to the river – but
Ross wasn't there.

He went to the tall trees —
but Ollie wasn't there.

That's strange.

Sid saw some footprints.

They were at the bushes
and the river too.

They weren't Spike's.

They weren't Ross's.

And they weren't Ollie's.

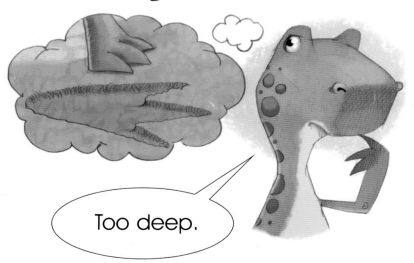

Sid followed the footprints.

The footprints led to...

...a huge dinosaur, called Rex.

P...p...please don't eat us, Rex.

Rex had taken Spike, Ross and Ollie home for dinner.

Sid wanted to scare Rex.
But did he have a roar?

There was only one way
to find out.

Sid crept up behind Rex.
He gave his biggest,
strongest, loudest...

ROAR!

Rex was terrified.

He ran off and didn't look
back.

"Three cheers for Sid!"
cried the others.

Hurray for Sid! His mighty roar saved us from that dinosaur.

Series editor:
Lesley Sims

First published in 2007 by Usborne Publishing Ltd., Usborne House,
83-85 Saffron Hill, London EC1N 8RT, England. www.usborne.com
Copyright © 2007 Usborne Publishing Ltd.

All rights reserved. No part of this publication may be reproduced,
stored in a retrieval system or transmitted in any form or by any
means, electronic, mechanical, photocopying, recording or otherwise
without the prior permission of the publisher. The name Usborne
and the devices ♀ ⊕ are Trade Marks of Usborne Publishing Ltd.
Printed in China. UE. First published in America in 2007.